THE SACRED ACT OF DEVOURING

by Samantha Oty

THE SACRED ACT OF DEVOURING

SPECIAL NOTE

Anyone receiving permission to produce THE SACRED ACT OF DEVOURING is required to give credit to the Author as sole and exclusive Author of the Play on the title page of all programs distributed in connection with performances of the Play and in all instances in which the title of the Play appears for purposes of advertising, publicizing or otherwise exploiting the Play and/or a production thereof. The name of the Author must appear on a separate line, in which no other name appears, immediately beneath the title and in size of type equal to 50% of the size of the largest, most prominent letter used for the title of the Play. No person, firm, or entity may receive credit larger or more prominent than that accorded the Author.

SPECIAL NOTE ON COVER ART FOR PROMOTION

Anyone receiving permission to produce THE SACRED ACT OF DEVOURING may use the cover art of this book for promotional purposes ONLY if they acquire the original graphics from Ghost Light Publications by adding on the graphics package during the licensing process.

Cover Art Design: Tiphiknee De Herrera
Book Design: Jonathan Cook
First Edition: July 2025
ISBN 978-1-964045-12-2

THE SACRED ACT OF DEVOURING received its World premiere at Madlab Theatre in Columbus, Ohio in October 2021 (under the original title LET'S HOPE YOU FEEL BETTER). It was directed by Sarah Vargo.

The cast was as follows:

THERESE .... McLane Nagy
TOBY .... John Grote
WREN .... Sha-Lemar Davis
ISAAC..Tom Murdock
ARCHIE .... Sean Taylor
MARIE ....Catherine Cryan Erney
DETECTIVE BASS.......................Duncan McKinnie

The crew was as follows:

SET DESIGN .... Kate Hawthorne
LIGHTING DESIGN .... Kurt Mueller
CONSTRUCTION LEAD.....................Ryan Harrison
BOOTH OPERATOR.........................Amanda Iman

"We all wear masks, and the time comes when we cannot remove them without removing some of our own skin."
— André Berthiaume

THE SACRED ACT OF DEVOURING

CHARACTERS

THERESE BLANC
A woman in her mid-20s. Usually the last to laugh at a joke. Loves a red lip.

TOBY MILLER
A man in his mid-to-late-20s. The charming boy next door.

ISAAC ABRAMS
A man in his late 20s to early 40s. Stuck in time.

WREN
A woman in her mid-20s. The Judy Greer of the group.

ARCHIE
A man in his mid-20s. Not as funny as he thinks he is.

MARIE BLANC
A woman in her early 50s Therese's French, intimidating mother.

DETECTIVE BASS
Man or woman in his/her late 30s.

SETTING

Therese's and Isaac's apartments.

The set is divided into two uneven sections. The larger half is Therese's apartment, a Pinterest worthy manor while the smaller is Isaac's, a dump.

Directors should feel free to have Isaac in his apartment even if he has no lines in the scene, so the weight of his absence can be felt in Act II.

TIME

Present.

OTHER ODDS AND ENDS

Soft transitions showing the passage of time should be utilized in between scenes until the blackout at intermission and the end. Directors are encouraged to have fun with this so long as it stays in tone with the rest of the play.

Therese's research monologues can be live or pre-recorded.

Underwear and sex scenes should be done at the comfort of the actors.

ACT 1

SCENE 1

An apartment that probably costs more than you make in a month.

Therese Blanc enters, dressed in a tank top and underwear. She's humming to herself as a new ring glistens on her left ring finger. Think Going to the Chapel or maybe a wedding march in the public domain.

She's a perfectionist, admiring how her new ring looks against the items in her apartment. As she ensures everything is in the best position. Better Homes and Garden perfection. The only thing out of place is a stack of textbooks on the coffee table.

She takes a picture of the ring with her camera. She's disappointed about something. The ring is too big on her finger.

Enter Toby from the bedroom.

TOBY. *(groggy)* What are you doing?

THERESE. Getting my camera. I'm going to document every moment of our engagement.

TOBY. Seriously?

THERESE. I want our children to be able to look back and see what their mommy and daddy were like before they let themselves go.

TOBY. *(placing his hands on her hips, pulling her closer)* And you think now is the best time to start.

THERESE. *(snapping a picture)* I think Addison and Marzia

deserve to see what Daddy's bedhead looked like.

TOBY. What if we have a boy?

THERESE. Addison *is* a boy's name.

(Therese takes another picture as he pulls her in for a kiss.)

Oh, morning breath-- *(grimacing)* Morning breath.

TOBY. Well, you have the rest of your life to get used to it.

THERESE. Or, I could leave the mouthwash by the bed.

(Toby crosses over to the kitchen and starts making coffee. Therese examines the ring.)

I really couldn't be happier.

TOBY. Mmmmhmm, what's wrong?

THERESE. Nothing.

TOBY. I know that face.

THERESE. *(sighs)* It's just a little big.

TOBY. So, we'll get it resized.

THERESE. It's just I've envisioned this moment for my entire life and the ring always fit--

TOBY. Therese, it's fine. Not everything needs to be perfect.

THERESE. You're right. We're getting married. That's more than enough.

(They share a kiss as someone begins pounding on the door. Therese crosses to answer it.)

TOBY. Leave it.

THERESE. It's Wren.

(She opens the door.)

WREN. Unbelievable! My best friend gets engaged, and I have to find out via a DM from none other than that piece of shit, waste of space, ginger freak Archie--

THERESE. Good morning.

WREN. Honestly, I'm so offended I don't think I even *want*

to be your Maid of Honor. You clearly hate me--Hello, Tobias--Clearly, you do not value our friendship. Our sisterhood, the pledge we took together our freshman year at BU when we were both scared little girls entering the cold, unforgiving world on our own.

(Therese walks into the bedroom as Wren continues her rant.)

We needed each other then, but now you have Toby, I guess there's no room for me anymore!

(Therese re-enters wearing jeans and pulling on a jacket. She crosses to the kitchen to pour her own cup of coffee.)

THERESE. Are you finished?

WREN. Yeah, I mean, I have more written down, but I didn't get a chance to rehearse it before getting here.

THERESE. I was going to call you this morning…if you gave me a chance.

WREN. I mean, Toby had time to tell Archie. Show me the ring.

(As Therese walks back over to the couch, hand extended.)

THERESE. It's too big.

WREN. So, get it resized. Ready to celebrate?

(Wren pulls a bottle of champagne out from her purse.)

TOBY. It's eight in the morning.

WREN. Then get me some orange juice and we'll call it brunch.

(She thrusts the bottle toward him.)

Open it. I'm scared.

THERESE. Still traumatized?

WREN. Macy had a black eye for a month.

(Toby begins working on the cork.)

Go over there. Shoo. *(full attention to Therese)* So, how did he do it? Tell me *everything*. Well, maybe not *everything*.

THERESE. Well, he surprised me with a gorgeous dinner out by the water, and he asked right before the dessert course.

WREN. That's it? *(to Toby)* That's *it*?

TOBY. Yeah, that's it. She said 'yes' didn't she?

THERESE. It was perfect. I never wanted the whole fanfare. It should be an intimate moment that's just the two of us. And the ring should fit.

TOBY. What do you want from me? I had to get the measurement while you were asleep.

THERESE. Your best is all I can ever ask of you.

WREN. Well, as sweet as that is, you should have parachuted from a helicopter in a tuxedo. Or gotten enough pugs to spell out "will you marry me".

TOBY. Where would I get sixteen pugs?

THERESE. Or a helicopter?

WREN. I could wrangle up some pugs.

(Toby's pager goes off.)

TOBY. Shit.

THERESE. You're on call?

TOBY. Yeah, I couldn't get anyone to take my shift. I have to take this, especially if I want to to attend that medical conference in Vegas in a couple weeks.

THERESE. Barely engaged twelve hours and you're already planning a trip.

TOBY. You know how important networking is.

THERESE. I know, I know…

(Toby heads into the bedroom to change out of his pajamas.)

WREN. That's life when you're married to a doctor, right? Knew it was coming.

THERESE. I'm a doctor as well, Wren.

WREN. Almost. Gotta get through that dissertation still. Get those clinic hours.

THERESE. It's fine. When duty calls, it's up to us to answer. They are our patients after all, deserving of the best care. Doesn't mean we can't celebrate. Brunch?

WREN. Please? I'm starving. Should we invite the girls? Does anyone else know yet?

THERESE. Just you and Archie.

TOBY. *(offstage)* She hasn't even told her mom yet.

(Therese pours Toby's coffee in a to-go mug. Like the perfect wife.)

THERESE. You know Maman and I don't have that kind of relationship.

WREN. A normal one?

THERESE. Define "normal".

WREN. It just might be nice to have your mom around for this huge life event.

(Toby returns to the living room wearing his scrubs.)

TOBY. Personally, I'm fine keeping Marie at a distance.

THERESE. And that's why I'm going to marry you.

WREN. All right, fine, but don't say I didn't try. Should I invite Macy and Jennifer?

THERESE. Yes, but don't tell them anything yet. I want to see the look on their faces.

TOBY. I'm out.

(Therese offers him the coffee cup and they exchange a brief kiss. Toby exits.)

(A spotlight appears on the other side of the stage in Isaac's apartment. There's an easel with the beginnings

of a painting. Perhaps it's Therese, it's hard to tell because he doesn't have all the details yet. She's still an outline to him. Isaac enters with a jar of paint to match the color of her hair, he's careful as he begins filling it in.)

WREN. All right, text message sent. Macy never turns down day drinking. Anyway, now that Toby's gone… isn't there something you want to ask me?

THERESE. Do you want to go to the library later to help with my dissertation?

WREN. Absolutely not. That's why I dropped out of the program. I'll leave the murder and cannibalism to you.

THERESE. Did you manage to find a home for that retriever?

WREN. Oh, great, that's so less bleak. And yeah, she was an angel and only an idiot would refuse to adopt her.

THERESE. Those were all my questions then.

WREN. Seriously? Do you want me to beg?

THERESE. For what?

WREN. Oh my god, you're insufferable.

THERESE. Wren… will you be my Maid of Honor?

WREN. Oh, Therese Blanc! It would be my privilege.

(Toby enters the apartment, frazzled.)

TOBY. Made it all the way to the T before I realized I forgot my wallet.

(Toby enters the bedroom.)

THERESE. You'd forget your head if it wasn't connected to your shoulders.

WREN. Did you just try to make a joke?

THERESE. It happens sometimes.

WREN. Don't. It's weird.

(Toby returns.)

WREN. Guess who's Maid of Honor?

TOBY. Hey, that's great, I already asked Archie to be my Best Man!

(They laugh at Wren's disdain as Therese's cell phone rings. Isaac is calling her.)

ISAAC. I know this is against the rules… but I can't get you… us… out of my head. Call me tonight, when you get the chance.

End of scene.

SCENE 2

Later that night.
Therese is in the depth of her research, speaking
into her phone to record her notes. She's sitting
at the open window, smoking a cigarette.

THERESE. Consensual Homicide refers to a homicide in which the victim was a willing participant in the act… often seeking out someone to assist them. While legal forms of consensual homicide exist within the United States and parts of Europe, it's only done so in cases dealing with terminally ill patients. Moving forward with the legalization is slow moving as there are many ethical concerns… see Jack Kevorkian. However, what if there is no terminal illness involved and the deceased simply wish… to die? Where is the line drawn between homicide and--

(Her phone rings, breaking her concentration. Isaac.)
You're breaking the rules. Again.

ISAAC. I know, but I'm working on this painting and I--I don't know what color blue to use. What color are your eyes?

THERESE. It's eight o'clock. You're only allowed to call me after midnight.

ISAAC. I know--I just… I wanted to hear your voice again.

THERESE. They're light blue. Borderline gray. Does that help?

ISAAC. Yeah--I think it does.

THERESE. Was there anything else?

ISAAC. Coke or Pepsi?

THERESE. What kind of question is that? Coke.

ISAAC. And what if the restaurant we went to only served Pepsi?

THERESE. We would go somewhere else.

(Beat.)

Are we going to hell for this?

ISAAC. No.

THERESE. Really? Catholicism looks down pretty harshly on this.

ISAAC. Well, good thing I'm not Catholic. I was always taught hell wasn't something to be scared of... it's a way to cleanse yourself of the sins you didn't atone for before you die.

THERESE. That's actually comforting.

(Beat.)

ISAAC. It's not easy, you know. The waiting. I want to see you.

THERESE. I want to see you too, but there's still so much to plan.

ISAAC. What else is there? We've been talking about this for three months. You're not getting cold feet are you?

THERESE. Of course not. I want this more than anything in the world. You. Me. Us. It's just--

(She looks at her ring. Still too big and perhaps a little too heavy.)

I'm engaged. The Boyfriend proposed last night.

ISAAC. The fuck? Don't you think this is something you should have told me--

THERESE. There are other things in my life that take precedence over our relationship.

ISAAC. Not for me--how is this going to work now?

THERESE. Don't worry about it. Everything is going to be fine.

ISAAC. Then set a date.

THERESE. Fine. Two weeks.

ISAAC. Two weeks.

THERESE. If everything works out, he's going to be leaving for a medical conference in Vegas. We'll have the whole weekend to ourselves.

ISAAC. And if he doesn't go?

THERESE. I'll come up with a backup plan. Trust me, everything will be perfect. It has to be… we only get one shot at this.

(Keys rattle outside the door as Toby returns home.)

I have to call you back.

(She hangs up and hides her cigarette, fanning smoke out the window as Toby opens the door.)

Sweets, I wasn't expecting you back this early.

TOBY. Nice to see you too.

THERESE. You just startled me. I was just recording some notes.

TOBY. Oh, sorry. Did you make anything for dinner?

THERESE. I ordered some takeout. The leftovers are in the fridge.

TOBY. Damn, I was hoping for something homemade.

THERESE. Well, Thai Express is my specialty. You know that.

(Therese's phone rings. A furious Isaac on the other end.)

TOBY. You gonna get that?

THERESE. Oh, it's just Macy. Probably some boy troubles. She's already stressed about finding a wedding date. You know how she is.

TOBY. Ah, right. Hey, I ran into Penny today and she told me that she and Rachel love living in Somerset.

THERESE. Oh? Are you planning on moving?

TOBY. Not yet, but I thought that we could start looking around after the wedding.

THERESE. That we don't even have a date for.

TOBY. Mom said she emailed our church for available dates, and she's waiting for them to get back to her.

THERESE. Wow, a church wedding and a house and Somerset. Any other decisions about my life that I should know?

TOBY. Come on, we've talked about this. You know I don't want to raise our kids in the city. They deserve to have a backyard.

THERESE. We can find a brownstone with a yard. And a church wedding? I thought we would keep it simple with a ceremony at the harbor.

TOBY. Guess we really need to sit down and start talking about this, huh?

THERESE. I guess we do.

(Both are confused about how they're nowhere near the same page.)

TOBY. Mom's dreamt of her boys getting married in the same church she got married in since she gave birth.

THERESE. And Maman would never step foot in a protestant church.

TOBY. So, we agree on the venue then?

THERESE. Come on, Toby, you know I'm not really a church girl. It wouldn't feel right. Besides, it's not like you're getting up early every Sunday to Praise the Lord.

TOBY. I know, but it's our wedding, and I just feel like it's the right thing to do.

THERESE. Fine. I respect your feelings. However, if I give you this, I don't want to hear any whining about what I want.

TOBY. Sounds like a deal. You know more about flowers than I do anyway.

(He gives her a kiss on the cheek.)

I'm gonna shower before bed. Join me?

THERESE. Sure. Just a minute.

(Toby exits.)

(into her phone) Research religion in regards to consensual homicide. Crucifixion… martyrdom… the saints… I'm sure there's something there.

(She then redials Isaac, glancing over her shoulder. He doesn't answer. Lost in his painting. Or maybe he's just pissed at her.)

Hey. I'm… I should have let you know about the engagement earlier, but it's going to be fine. I still want this as long as you do.

(She hangs up and exits.)

End of scene.

SCENE 3

The next morning there's a knock at the door.
Toby, dressed for basketball practice, enters
from the bedroom to answer it.
Enter Archie, Toby's piece of shit, ginger friend.
He's also ready for some b-ball.

ARCHIE. Pack your bags. We're in.

TOBY. In what?

ARCHIE. Check your email. Doctor Roberts picked us to go
with him to the Vegas medical conference. Two weeks.

TOBY. Oh, shit, that's awesome. I don't know if now's the
best time to go--

ARCHIE. Why not?

(Pause.)

Oh, right. Congratulations. Meant to text you yesterday.
But it's not like I didn't know about it.

TOBY. Thanks. Your sincerity knows no bounds.

ARCHIE. The conference. Are you pumped?

TOBY. Definitely, yeah. Just need to talk to Therese and
make sure she's fine with it.

ARCHIE. She's your fiancée, not your mom.

TOBY. It's still nice to ask. Think about other people.

ARCHIE. That's why I'm staying single.

(Enter Wren through the main door.)

WREN. *(to Archie)* Ew. *(to Toby)* Is she awake yet? We're
supposed to hit the gym.

TOBY. Working on it. She was up late last night working
on stuff.

(Archie picks up a book from the stack on the counter.)

ARCHIE. "Beyond Any Kind of God" by Jack Kevorkian. Just, you know, some light reading, right?

WREN. You are so annoying. She's getting a PhD, what do you expect?

ARCHIE. Forgive me for being concerned about who my best friend might be committing his life to. *Commit* being the key word.

TOBY. He's just cranky this morning. Drink some coffee.

(Therese enters, speaking French into her cell phone.)

THERESE. Non, maman. Laisse-moi vérifier mon calendrier.

(She crosses over to her purse, where her day planner is hiding. She begins rattling off dates.)

ARCHIE. What's that about?

WREN. French. Can only mean it's Madame Marie Blanc.

TOBY. Probably about their monthly lunch in New York.

(Things are starting to get heated on the phone.)

THERESE. J'ai aussi une vie. Je ne peux pas continuer à me plier à ce que tu veux quand tu veux--

(She exits into the bedroom.)

WREN. You've met her, right?

TOBY. Uh, briefly, at, uh, graduation?

ARCHIE. That was six years ago.

TOBY. She likes to keep Marie on a need-to-know basis. They do lunch once a month. It works for them.

WREN. It's amazing she's so well adjusted.

(Archie scoffs.)

What?

ARCHIE. You're telling me she's never put a hamster in a microwave.

TOBY. That's my future wife.

ARCHIE. And I'm so happy for you.

(Therese returns, frazzled. She begins packing books into her bookbag as everyone watches her.)

THERESE. What?

WREN. How's Marie?

THERESE. Marie is great, thrilled that her poupée is to be wed.

(She sees the book in Archie's hand and yanks it away.)
Give me that.

ARCHIE. What the hell are you studying anyway?

THERESE. Consensual homicide.

ARCHIE. Murder?

THERESE. *(unamused)* Is it still murder if the victim asked for it?

TOBY. Yes.

THERESE. *(to Toby)* I'm taking the train to New York next Saturday. She's excited to start planning the wedding.

TOBY. Did you mention the Methodist church?

THERESE. Of course not, darling, I'm planning to wait until she's finished a bottle of her favorite Pinot Noir.

ARCHIE. How the hell can murder be consensual.

WREN. Like assisted suicide dumbass.

THERESE. Which is legal in ten states and the District of Columbia, but only in cases where the patient is terminal. "Death with Dignity". But I'm more interested in cases outside of that. Instances where someone… simply wants to die. For example, Sharon Lopatkas wanted to be tortured to death and Armin Meiwes found someone online who was eager and willing to be cannibalized.

ARCHIE. Do I need to keep an eye on Toby?

THERESE. If I wanted to kill him, I would have done it already.

TOBY. And I would probably deserve it.

ARCHIE. What do you think of all of this?

TOBY. I can't say I agree with it. We took an oath to do no harm.

THERESE. How is it doing harm if it's what the person wants? Wouldn't the harm then be to not euthanize?

WREN. Euthanize?

ARCHIE. We're talking about humans.

TOBY. If it were morally correct then Kevorkian would have never been convicted.

THERESE. Wrongfully.

WREN. Can we go, please?

ARCHIE. It's not up to us to decide when someone dies.

THERESE. Exactly, it's up to them. It's not like any of us had a choice on coming into the world, so we might as well have a say on how we leave it.

WREN. I'm leaving without you.

(Wren exits.)

THERESE. I'll see you later, sweets.

(She kisses Toby before following Wren.)

ARCHIE. You didn't tell her about Vegas.

TOBY. You didn't give me a chance. I'll talk to her tonight.

ARCHIE. If you get the chance.

(He mimes stabbing someone.)

End of Scene.

SCENE 4

Later that evening.
Toby is getting dinner ready when Therese walks
through the door.

THERESE. Well, this is a nice surprise.

TOBY. I cook all the time.

THERESE. For your other girlfriend?

TOBY. Fiancé.

THERESE. *(gasp)* You're engaged? When were you going
to tell me?

TOBY. It's not my fault you're a better cook than me.

THERESE. All it takes is knowing how to read, my love.

TOBY. Hey, I'm sorry about Archie earlier.

THERESE. It's fine.

TOBY. We're just cut from the same cloth, ya know? We're
in this to save lives.

THERESE. And I'm not?

TOBY. That's not what I--

THERESE. Toby, it's fine. Already forgotten. Really.

TOBY. I just don't want you to think I don't respect what
you're doing.
(Therese hugs him.)

THERESE. You don't need to apologize for your friends.
(He kisses the top of her head.)

TOBY. I do have an ulterior motive for making dinner
tonight.

THERESE. I knew it.

TOBY. I'm going to the medical conference in Las Vegas.

THERESE. Oh. That's all?

TOBY. Yes.

THERESE. Okay. When is it?

TOBY. Two weeks.

THERESE. Two weeks? I don't see any problems with that.

TOBY. Really?

THERESE. Why would I have a problem with that? It's for work.

TOBY. Archie's going too.

THERESE. Ah. Well, still, it's fine.

TOBY. You're not upset I'm leaving while we're planning the wedding?

THERESE. Who's planning anything right now? I haven't even had a chance to look at the dates your mother sent. October seems like it would be a good time…

TOBY. Right. Also, I was talking with her earlier, and my cousin Mallory wants to be our planner. For free. Well, not free. In exchange for a testimonial.

THERESE. Which one's Mallory again?

TOBY. The one I grew up with? Lives in Williamsburg now…

THERESE. The fat one?

TOBY. She's not fat.

THERESE. With the magenta bathroom?

TOBY. …Yes.

THERESE. Oh, god no.

TOBY. What's wrong with Mallory?

THERESE. Her throw pillows. Her wallpaper. The lettuce earrings?

TOBY. We can't use that to determine whether or not she'd do a good job.

(Toby pulls Therese into his arms in an attempt to

romance her.)

She's free and you'll get to boss her around. You love bossing people around.

THERESE. I can afford a wedding planner.

TOBY. This is the last thing I'm asking for.

THERESE. Really? Because I'm going to hold you to it. I don't want to hear about your little cousin… Annabelle and her *need* to be a flower girl because her classmate was one.

TOBY. No kids at the wedding.

THERESE. Agreed.

TOBY. Finally. I wonder what else we can agree on?

THERESE. How good I look in that leather strappy thing you got me?

TOBY. Yeah, that's a good one.

(They kiss passionately--as though Therese is trying to consume him.)

(Consume.)

(Consume.)

(CONSUME.)

(Toby breaks the kiss abruptly.)

You bit me.

THERESE. I'm sorry--

TOBY. --I think it's bleeding--

THERESE. --I got carried away. I'm sorry.

(She holds his head in place to look at his lip.)

TOBY. It's okay.

(He kisses her again. They keep it gentle this time. Therese's phone rings. It's Isaac. They try to ignore it, but the second it's finished, he tries to call her again. Clearly, it's urgent. Toby reaches for the phone despite Therese's protests.)

Hello?

ISAAC. Uh… hi?

TOBY. Who's this?

ISAAC. This is… um...

TOBY. Are you one of Therese's students?

ISAAC. Uh… yes?

THERESE. Who is it?

TOBY. Here she is.

(He hands her the phone and returns to the kitchen to put dinner in the fridge.)

THERESE. Hello? Professor Blanc speaking.

ISAAC. It's me…

TOBY. Meet you in the bedroom.

(Therese covers the mouthpiece of the phone as Toby gives her a kiss and a smack on the bum.)

THERESE. Put on the leather strappy thing.

(She waits for the door to close.)

Are you insane? You can't keep breaking the rules?

ISAAC. I'm sorry, I wasn't expecting your *fiancé* to answer.

THERESE. What do you want?

ISAAC. The other night. I'm sorry, I wasn't angry, I was just frustrated…

THERESE. I noticed. But I have good news. Two weeks. I just need to finalize some items on my end, but we should be able to meet in two weeks.

ISAAC. Wow, really?

THERESE. Are you excited?

ISAAC. I'm just ready, but I feel like you're just leading me on. And tonight… I was starting to think… about it.

THERESE. Is everything all right?

ISAAC. Everything's fine… I just--this feels weird, ya know?

THERESE. How so?

ISAAC. Well, why were you on the forum? Really.

(Therese glances over her shoulder.)

THERESE. I was there to do research for my dissertation.

ISAAC. Research.

THERESE. Well, I was just going to do it on serial killers and early warning signs. Then I found a couple cases of consensual homicide, and I couldn't get it out of my head.

ISAAC. So, *that's* why you were on the site?

THERESE. Yes, I was *researching* forums where people with these fantasies seek satisfaction. You, however, seemed to be interested in a lot more than roleplaying. And here we are.

ISAAC. So… I'm just research? Long way to go to get an 'A'.

(Beat.)

THERESE. I--I just believe people have the right to decide how--and when they die.

ISAAC. I don't want to hurt.

THERESE. Okay. But, what you've asked for… all of that is going to--

ISAAC. I know. But the actual death part. That should be peaceful. By the time we're done… I think I'll have earned that.

THERESE. Of course.

(Isaac looks over the edge of the window and drops an empty beer can.)

ISAAC. What do you think would be the worst way to die?

THERESE. I don't have time--

ISAAC. Please?

THERESE. Jumping off a building. Or a bridge. Too much

time in between to change your mind.

ISAAC. *(looking down)* Good point.

(He rests his head against the windowsill.)

How are you going to do me?

THERESE. Interesting way to phrase it.

ISAAC. You know what I mean.

THERESE. I don't know. You want it painless, so I guess I'll have to look into it. And afterward--

ISAAC. Don't tell me. I don't care what happens to my body.

THERESE. Really?

ISAAC. Yeah, my body isn't me. My mind is me.

THERESE. I suppose that's a good way to look at it.

ISAAC. Can I ask you something? Since you're a therapist and all.

THERESE. What?

ISAAC. Do you think this is selfish? What we're doing?

THERESE. I don't really know. But, what do you think is more selfish, someone killing themselves or forcing someone to continue living in a world where they're completely miserable, just so you don't have to miss them?

ISAAC. I've never really thought about it that way. What about you? Is what you're going to do selfish?

THERESE. I don't know. I guess I'll find out, but I like to think I'm helping someone in need.

ISAAC. What happens to us when we die?

THERESE. God, that's the question isn't it? I don't know… I don't think anyone but the dead can answer that. I think that's why we have our religions--to give us some sense of closure about losing the ones we love.

ISAAC. Like, ghosts?

THERESE. Ghosts, reincarnations… Heaven… As much as I like to think there's something after we die, I really just think it's something we invented to cope with death.

ISAAC. Yeah, it's pretty terrifying to think that once you're gone that's it… you're just--

THERESE. Gone?

(Pause.)

You're not having second thoughts are you? It's fine if you are because I'd rather know now than later.

ISAAC. No… no.

(Beat.)

Hey.

THERESE. Yeah?

ISAAC. I'm really… happy I found you.

TOBY. *(from the bedroom)* Therese?

THERESE. I'm happy too… Oh..

ISAAC. Yeah?

THERESE. I'm coming to New York next weekend. I'm busy in the afternoon, but maybe we can meet in the evening.

ISAAC. I'd like that a lot.

THERESE. Really?

ISAAC. Yeah.

THERESE. And you're sure you're not having second thoughts? We can end it now.

ISAAC. No, I want to do this. I want to give you this.

THERESE. Promise?

ISAAC. I promise.

(She hangs up and retreats into the bedroom.)

THERESE. Sorry, my advisor had some questions.

End of Scene

SCENE 4b

Therese is talking into her phone. Rambling off notes.

THERESE. In the case of Armin Meiwes and Simon Brande, the encounter and end result were ultimately for sexual gratification. While it may be difficult to understand from an outside perspective why one would want to be brutalized in this way. A couple years earlier, Sharon Lopatka sought out someone to torture her to death. It's easy to look at the victim's past and come to a conclusion as to why they wanted their lives to end…but what about their killers? In both cases, the ones who committed the act of murder had no history of violence, yet they were still able to do what they did. Why did it take a willing victim to make them go through with it if this was something that was always in them. What sets them apart from a Bundy or a Wurnos? Why did they need the consent of their victims when they could have sought the satisfaction they needed at any time?

End of Scene

SCENE 5

Isaac is trying to find the right light for his painting when there's a knock at the door.
He opens it and takes a step back for Therese to enter.

ISAAC. I was waiting for you to call--

THERESE. I followed a neighbor inside.

ISAAC. Were the directions--

THERESE. Yes. They were great. I made it, right?

ISAAC. Do you want a drink?

THERESE. Wine?

ISAAC. I have beer.

THERESE. That's fine.

(Isaac walks over to a small mini fridge and pulls out a couple of beers. He hands one to Therese and sits on the edge of a ratty old recliner. Therese crosses the stage and sits on the edge of a dirty couch.)

ISAAC. I hope you're not driving.

THERESE. In New York? You should know better.

ISAAC. You're not what I was expecting. Younger. Prettier.

(Neither is sure what to do. After months of talking on the phone and online, they find themselves in uncharted territory. Isaac, however, is smitten with Therese. He is the one to break the silence.)

How was your afternoon? You said you had lunch plans.

THERESE. I did, yes. I was supposed to, but she didn't show up.

ISAAC. I'm sorry.

THERESE. It's fine. Not like it was a surprise, I was just hoping that maybe…

ISAAC. What?

THERESE. Nothing. I shouldn't be telling you all this.

ISAAC. It's fine, who would I tell?

THERESE. I was just hoping that maybe we could have a normal day together. Go to lunch, go shopping--I even made an appointment at Kleinfeld to try on wedding dresses… but she didn't come.

ISAAC. That must suck.

THERESE. It does. All of that must sound so trivial to you.

ISAAC. If there's one thing I've learned bartending is that we all have our own issues. Who cares if yours are of the first world variety.

THERESE. Fuck you.

(They laugh. She sees the painting.)

Is this it?

ISAAC. Yeah, but now that you're here, maybe I should redo it. It doesn't do you justice.

(Pause.)

THERESE. No, I suppose there is something missing. Hmm… "we all have our own issues".

ISAAC. We do.

THERESE. My father killed himself when I was a little girl. And I was the one who found him in the bathtub. My piano lesson was canceled that day, so I was home before the nanny or Maman. The water was pink… but it was still warm. Sometimes I wonder if I did something… called someone… if he would still be alive. Maman was appalled when she came home and found me sitting by the bathtub.

(Pause.)

And a week later I shoved my mom's cat out of the

window. Second story.

ISAAC. Cry for help?

THERESE. An experiment. To see if I could do it. Just because. Maybe I was a little sad about my father and wanted to seek out something in my life to control.

ISAAC. So, I'm not your first?

THERESE. I didn't start killing neighborhood animals if that's what you're thinking. I'm not a pyschopath.

ISAAC. I wasn't thinking anything.

THERESE.I just wanted to see if… it was fast… if he felt anything.

ISAAC. There's a difference between being shoved out a window and slitting your wrists.

THERESE. I know that, but the results are the same. They were both probably afraid…and then calm before… nothingness. Finally at peace.

ISAAC. There's a lot of beauty in death.

THERESE. I'm so glad to finally have someone who understands.

ISAAC. You don't talk about this with your fiancé?

THERESE. Are you kidding? Don't get me wrong. I -- I love him. I'm going to marry him in the cutest little Methodist church and we're going to have a nice house with a white picket fence and I'll sacrifice my career to raise our two-point-five children. He wouldn't understand.

(Laughs.)

I don't think he's ever had a mischievous thought in his head. The kind that starts to eat away at you like a poison. Haunting every moment of your life. He just wouldn't understand any of this, and I don't think it's wrong to find someone who would -- Someone who can see the darkest parts of my mind and still want me.

Everyone deserves that and if I didn't find it in you… I don't know what would have happened. And that scares me.

(Isaac has taken out his paints and started touching up the painting. This annoys her.)

You have nothing to say?

ISAAC. I'm just taking it all in. But, I see it now. What it's missing.

(Therese stands and looks around his sad, small apartment. She feels sorry for him.)

THERESE. It's a shame. Your art is going to be worth a lot more after you're gone.

ISAAC. 'Tis the fate of many great artists. There's already a plan in place.

THERESE. Oh, really?

ISAAC. This isn't the first time I've tried. All my ducks are in a row.

THERESE. Oh?

ISAAC. Not like what we're doing. I tried it by myself, but I couldn't get past the… fear.

THERESE. Is that why you were looking for someone to do it for you?

ISAAC. Yeah, if I can get someone to do the hard part then I get to reap the benefits.

(Therese picks up a picture frame off the shelf and holds it up.)

THERESE. Who's this?

ISAAC. My niece, Abby.

THERESE. Looks like she adores you.

(She puts the frame back in its place. She lingers on it, her expression slowly changing, panicked. There's someone out there who cares about him.)

Oh my god, what are we doing?

(She grabs her purse from the chair and heads toward the door.)

ISAAC. Where are you going?

(She tries to leave, but Isaac grabs her arm and pulls her back.)

THERESE. We can't do this. I can't help you die knowing there's someone who'll miss you.

ISAAC. *(holding her by the shoulders)* That picture was taken ten years ago.

THERESE. What?

ISAAC. This isn't the first time I've tried to kill myself. After the first time… I was staying with them and tried it again. She found me and they wanted nothing to do with me afterwards. She doesn't remember me, but I have it in my will that if anything happens to me, she's the beneficiary. Of everything. My life insurance, my art sales. I want to make it up to her. If I do one thing right in my life, I'm going to ensure her happiness.

(Therese drops her purse onto the couch. Isaac takes his hands off her shoulders.)

THERESE. This isn't normal.

ISAAC. What is?

THERESE. You don't get it… it's not just assisted suicide or whatever we want to call it. We're talking about ending your life, and I'm getting off on the high it'll bring.

(She sits on the couch and Isaac joins her.)

ISAAC. It is like playing God.

THERESE. Exactly.

ISAAC. I don't care if what we have is normal… I like it, and I like you.

(Music like "Your Love" by The Outfield begins to play

Therese sets down her beer and stands.)

THERESE. I love this song.

ISAAC. You're not old enough to love this song.

THERESE. Good music knows no age. I wanted this song to be our first dance. But Toby vetoed. He thinks it's sad. Not romantic.

ISAAC. We don't need to talk about him right now.

(Therese sets down her drink and dances to the music. Letting loose for the first time this play. Have fun. Be a little silly. Forget why they're meeting. Do what you want, but the dance should end with Isaac dipping Therese.)

THERESE. *(smiles)* Je pourrais tomber amoureux de toi.

ISAAC. What's that mean?

THERESE. It's just a stupid French saying.

ISAAC. I want a beautiful death.

THERESE. I'll do my best.

(He leans in to steal a kiss. She's surprised, but not mad.)

ISAAC. Let's do it tonight.

(The moment is ruined. Therese pushes him away.)

THERESE. Don't be ridiculous.

ISAAC. Why not? I'm ready and you're here. I can't wait anymore.

THERESE. You'll have to. The timing isn't right. It needs to be perfect. I followed a neighbor inside.

ISAAC. I don't fucking get you.

THERESE. Excuse me?

ISAAC. Why did you want to come here tonight if you didn't want to do it?

THERESE. I thought it would be nice to meet before the time comes. So we're not complete strangers when I--I don't know what you want from me. I don't know the rules.

ISAAC. You're the one making them.

THERESE. I can't do it tonight because *I'm* not ready. I can't ki--I can't help you and then go home to Toby. It's just all wrong right now.

(Isaac puts an arm around her. She leans into him.)

But maybe there is something we can do tonight… to keep us both satisfied?

(Isaac thinks for a second before walking to his easel and returning with an exacto knife. Or any sharp object.)

ISAAC. I've never been able to see a future for myself… I've tried to create five-year plans, therapy everything, but it's just been empty. Until I found you. You're my lighthouse in an endless sea. I'm not going to let you down. I really want to make you happy.

(He places the blade in her hand before pulling off his shirt. She stares at the knife, taking a moment to herself. Then, she drags it across his chest leaving a trail of blood. Therese looks at the blood on her hand and at the painting. She stands and crosses over to it. Isaac stands to look at what she's done. Without a word, they kiss--passionately, as though Therese is trying to consume him.)

(Consume.)

(Consume.)

(CONSUME.)

(He bends her over the table. As it happens, Therese reaches over to the painting to smear his blood across her painted face.)

End of Scene

SCENE 5b

The stage is still black as Therese's phone rings.

ISAAC. Who is it?

THERESE. Toby.

ISAAC. Ignore it.

> *(The phone stops ringing as the lights return. They're laying together on the couch. Therese lights a cigarette and sits in his chair.)*

What're you going to do with my skull?

THERESE. *(smirks)* I thought you didn't care what happens to your body? Your soul is what matters? Your body is just the *physical vessel*?

ISAAC. I'm curious.

THERESE. Curiosity killed the cat.

ISAAC. But satisfaction brought it back... we always leave that line out.

THERESE. I haven't thought about that. Maybe grind it up with the rest of your bones and use it to make bread. I think I'll use the other parts of you for a hearty steak dinner. Barbeque? There's going to be a lot of meat...

ISAAC. You could make it into an ashtray.

THERESE. I don't smoke.

> *(Pause.)*

Unless I'm stressed--I don't smoke unless I'm stressed. I quit for Toby.

ISAAC. Fuck Toby.

> *(Isaac takes the cigarette from her.)*

THERESE. That's not very nice... I love Toby.

ISAAC. What is love if you can't even tell him you smoke?

THERESE. I don't smoke.

(Pause.)

You know, in some ancient civilizations, they used to practice cannibalism because they thought they could inherit someone's strength.

ISAAC. Is that what you want? My strength?

THERESE. No… I used to think it was about power. Taking control over another person, peeling the flesh off their bones until there's nothing left…

(She reaches for his hand, tracing the lines of his palm.)

Now, I think it's more than that. I like the thought that when it's all over, you're going to be a part of me. That there's always going to be some part of you that exists within me and that I'll never really be alone.

(She bites his hand. Hard.)

(Beat.)

THERESE. It really is a beautiful painting.

(Pause.)

I should go. My train leaves early--

ISAAC. Yeah, yeah, you have an early meeting.

(He stands up to assist Therese with her coat. He leads her to the door.)

THERESE. My family has a cabin up north. Totally secluded. In one week… I'll take you there.

ISAAC. One week.

(They hug.)

THERESE. You should destroy that before you come. Burn it.

(She exits. Isaac looks at the painting, smiling. How could he destroy something so beautiful?)

End of Scene

SCENE 6

*A giant bouquet of flowers sits on the counter in
Therese's apartment.*

*Toby is laying on the couch eating a bag of chips
and playing a game on a system. Therese enters
the apartment, and he jumps up, hiding the chips
behind one of the throw pillows and putting his
drink on a coaster.*

THERESE. What's the occasion? You only get me flowers
if you have a coupon.

TOBY. Flowers? Oh, no, I didn't get those for you, someone
else sent them.

*(Setting her suitcase on the ground, Therese crosses to
the flowers.)*

THERESE. Did you read the card?

TOBY. They aren't my flowers.

*(Therese digs through the mass of flowers to find the
small white envelope. She opens it and reads the note.)*

THERESE. *(French accent)* "Sorry, ma poupée, maybe next
time? Much love, Maman."

(She rips the card in half.)

TOBY. She didn't come to lunch? Why didn't you tell me?

THERESE. It doesn't matter. It's just ridiculous because if
the roles were reversed, I'd never hear the end of it.

TOBY. Come here.

*(He sits on the couch and motions for her to join him.
She does so.)*

THERESE. What?

TOBY. I just want to look at you. I missed you.

THERESE. You're so corny.

TOBY. You're glowing.

THERESE. Don't be stupid. People don't glow.

TOBY. You do. You always light up the room.

THERESE. Do you want something?

TOBY. Can't a man compliment his bride?

THERESE. Of course. But it feels like you want something.

TOBY. I've been thinking… we've both been busy and haven't really had a chance to spend time alone since the engagement. So, maybe we could do a weekend getaway to your family's cabin soon?

THERESE. Cabin?

TOBY. Yeah, it'll give us a chance to re-connect and be together… no interruptions… just the two of us…

THERESE. I don't think the cabin is a good idea.

TOBY. Why not?

THERESE. It's hardly been used over the last couple years, so I don't think it'll be an ideal romantic getaway.

TOBY. Can you ask Marie to have it cleaned?

THERESE. Seriously?

TOBY. Right. Maybe not the best time.

THERESE. *(sighs)* But, maybe. I'll see what I can do.

TOBY. Awesome.

THERESE. Are you excited for your trip this weekend?

TOBY. Should be a good time. Good presentations.

THERESE. Make a list so you don't forget anything.

TOBY. Yeah, I'll get right on that. But how was the trip other than getting stood up?

THERESE. New York was good.

TOBY. Just "good"? Did you go dress shopping?

THERESE. Alone?

TOBY. Might explain why you're glowing.

THERESE. I canceled the appointment. It's fine. There's still time. Wedding's not until October, so there's still time.

TOBY. All right… but that doesn't explain why you're glowing.

THERESE. I'm not glowing.

(Toby reaches for the camera on the table.)

Stop that.

TOBY. "I want to document every moment of our engagement."

(He takes her picture and sets the camera aside. He leans in and starts kissing her face.)

THERESE. Okay… okay…

(He moves on to her neck.)

All right. That's enough affection for now.

(She stands up and crosses to the kitchen.)

Are there going to be strippers?

TOBY. Huh?

THERESE. In Vegas. Your trip. Are you two going to any strip clubs?

TOBY. I'm not planning to go to any strip clubs. What's wrong? Do you not want me to go?

(She takes a seat on the couch again.)

THERESE. I want you to go, Toby. Just promise you'll be honest about anything that happens?

TOBY. Of course, I'll even text you every five minutes so you know I'm behaving.

THERESE. I want you to be happy. I hope you know that.

TOBY. Well, I hope you would. It would make things a little awkward if you didn't.

(Therese laughs.)

Anything else?

THERESE. I'm fine, I promise. Just know that I trust you.

TOBY. And I trust you… you're the love of my life.

THERESE. Good. Did you check the mail today?

TOBY. I can.

THERESE. Please.

(He kisses her cheek and begins to exit.)

TOBY. Do you want to order Chinese for dinner? Or Thai?

THERESE. I'm kind of in the mood for Italian. Pizza?

TOBY. I'm cool with that.

(He exits. Therese crosses to her suitcase and pulls out the T-shirt stained in Isaac's blood. She stares at it for a moment before holding it to her face and inhales.)

End of Scene

SCENE 6b

Therese's notes.

THERESE. Consumption. We love to consume. Gorge ourselves to satisfy our hunger. Our vanity. Our needs. So, why would it be so wrong for us to consume to satisfy our desire when the very act of sexual pleasure is inherently cannibalistic. We consume each other when we kiss, when we perform oral, and the act of penetration is itself an act of consumption. Should it really be that shocking that one would wish to consume another person… to hold them with you forever?

End of Scene.

SCENE 7

Stage remains dark.
Therese's voice is heard. Not recorded. She's
been crying.

THERESE. God, I am heartily sorry for having offended you, and I detest all my sins because I dread the loss of heaven and the pains of hell; but most of all because they offend you, my God, who are all good and deserving of all my love. I firmly resolve with the help of your grace to confess my sins, do penance, and to amend my life. Amen.

(Lights rise.)

(Therese is sitting on the floor of the living room, prayer beads in hand. A week has passed without incident, and Toby is about to leave on his trip. She's been crying. Toby enters dragging his suitcase behind him.)

TOBY. You're still up?

THERESE. Not tired.

TOBY. I don't think I've ever seen you pray before.

THERESE. Doesn't happen a lot.

TOBY. Are you all right?

THERESE. Yeah, I think the stress of the wedding… and my research is starting to take its toll.

TOBY. Is that all?

THERESE. What do you mean?

TOBY. You were pretty upset when Marie didn't make it to lunch.

THERESE. That was a week ago.

TOBY. But you two haven't talked about it--

THERESE. We don't need to talk.

TOBY. Should I cancel?

THERESE. No! No… go. I'm fine.

TOBY. Are you sure?

THERESE. Remember your resident days? Sometimes we just need days to… wallow in self pity. I'll be back to normal by the time you get back.

(There's a knock on the door.)

ARCHIE. *(offstage)* Let's go! The meter's running.

TOBY. Okay.

(He kisses the top of her head and crosses to the door.)

I love you.

THERESE. I know…

End of Scene.

SCENE 8

The door buzzes. Therese, in a robe, hurries to answer.

THERESE. Yes?

ISAAC. It's me.

THERESE. Oh, God. You're early.

(She buzzes him up anyway and returns to her bedroom to change. After a moment, there's a knock at the door. She rushes out, adjusting the dress as she goes.)

Hi.

ISAAC. Hi.

(He gives her a quick peck on the cheek as she lets him in.)

So, this is your place?

THERESE. *(wringing her hands nervously)* Yeah, this is it… the cabin is a couple hours north. Totally isolated. Everything is going to be perfect.

ISAAC. Great. So, how much does a place like this cost up here--if you don't mind my asking?

THERESE. Oh, I don't know… Maman pays for it. I think two thousand?

(The stove dings.)

Oh, the roast.

(She takes the wine bottle from Isaac and scurries over to the kitchen.)

ISAAC. Roast?

THERESE. *(taking the roast out of the oven)* Yes, I made us some dinner and appetizers… it's the least I could do.

ISAAC. Are you sure that's a good idea?

THERESE. Why wouldn't it be?

ISAAC. Well, I mean, I don't know how you're getting rid of my body but if it involves cutting me open… and if I die before I finish digesting… it might get a little messy-- *(chuckles)* Well, messier.

THERESE. Oh… oh… well… I guess we can just enjoy the smell then…

ISAAC. No, you go ahead and eat. I appreciate the thought though. It was really nice of you.

THERESE. No, I wouldn't be comfortable eating in front of you.
(They both sit on the edge of the couch. Therese stares out into space as Isaac pulls out vodka and cough syrup from a brown paper bag.)
What are those?

ISAAC. They're to make it easier on my end… put me right to sleep. I won't feel a thing, hopefully.

THERESE. I promised it wouldn't hurt--

ISAAC. And I believe you but… it's not the physical pain I'm worried about…

THERESE. Oh… right. You put a lot of thought into this.

ISAAC. Haven't you?

THERESE. Of course… just not about your end of the arrangement.
(Beat.)

ISAAC. So, Toby's gone for the weekend?

THERESE. Yeah, they left this morning… won't be back until Monday.

ISAAC. All right then…
(They're both silent and don't look at each other for a long time.)

THERESE. Isaac?

ISAAC. Yeah?

THERESE. I'm really glad it's you.

ISAAC. Yeah?

THERESE. Yeah… I think you're the only one who truly understands… understands why… why this is important to me.

ISAAC. I try my best.

THERESE. Sometimes, I think you understand me better than Toby.

ISAAC. Really?

THERESE. Really. Since we started talking I've wondered what it would have been like if we met under other circumstances… maybe things would have been different for us? It's silly because you haven't been in my life for that long but… I'm going to miss our conversations.

ISAAC. I feel the same way.

THERESE. You do?

(Isaac looks at her for the first time since they sat on the couch.)

ISAAC. Therese, I think you're the best thing that could ever happen to me. So, yeah, I wish things could have gone differently for us. I can't remember the last time someone cared about me the way you do.

(Isaac gently turns her face towards him and kisses her.)

(softly) I love you.

(Therese takes a deep breath and closes her eyes. Slowly, she stands.)

THERESE. Come on.

ISAAC. Where?

THERESE. Let's just enjoy our last night together.

(She heads toward the bedroom. But there's a knock at the door that makes them both freeze.)

WREN. *(offstage, drunk)* Rese… are you home?

THERESE. Shit.

(She shoves Isaac into the bedroom and yanks the door shut before letting Wren into the apartment.)

What's wrong?

WREN. I messed up.

THERESE. How?

WREN. I like Archie.

THERESE. What?

WREN. We've been texting because of the wedding and… I like him. He's not that bad.

THERESE. You came over to tell me that?

WREN. Yeah… Macy and I were at the bar, and I got sad because Archie's across the country--is that a roast? Why are you making a roast? It's like 10:00…

THERESE. Where's Macy?

WREN. She's downstairs bumming a smoke off some hot guy in your building.

THERESE. You should probably get back to her.

WREN. Do you want to come with us? I feel kind of bad you've been stuck inside all day doing homework.

THERESE. Really, it's fine. If I didn't like it then I wouldn't do it.

WREN. Still, you should come with us. Your husband-to-be is in Vegas doing god knows what--

THERESE. Wren. I really need you to go. I'm very busy and don't have time to go out tonight.

(Therese ushers her to the door.)

WREN. Okay… okay. No need to be a bitch about it.

THERESE. I'm sorry. Maybe we can get brunch on Sunday?

Some place with bottomless Bloody Marys?

WREN. Yes. Oh my god, yes.

THERESE. And, listen, if you really like Archie... for whatever reason... you should just let him know. But for the love of god don't break up before the wedding.

WREN. You're right. You're always so right about this kind of stuff.

(Wren's phone dings.)

Macy's about to go to another bar. Rude.

THERESE. Then you better hurry.

WREN. Okay, I love you.

(She forces Therese into a tight hug before exiting. Isaac emerges from the bedroom.)

ISAAC. Well, that was close.

THERESE. It's fine. She didn't notice anything.

ISAAC. She seemed nice.

THERESE. Please don't talk about her.

ISAAC. Sorry?

THERESE. She's part of my real life.

ISAAC. And I'm not?

THERESE. No--yes--you are. But by this time tomorrow, you won't be here anymore, and I'll have to go back to normal.

ISAAC. That easy, huh?

THERESE. I don't know. I don't want to fight.

(She takes his hands in hers.)

It's our last night together.

ISAAC. It doesn't have to be our last night.

THERESE. What?

ISAAC. What if this doesn't need to be our last night?

THERESE. I don't get what you're saying... are you changing your mind?

ISAAC. What if I am?

THERESE. *(beginning to panic)* No, no, no, no. You can't.
(She starts wringing her hands, anxiously.)

ISAAC. It's okay. Let's stay calm.

THERESE. No, no, *you promised*!

ISAAC. I'm sorry, but you've said since the beginning that I'm allowed to change my mind.

THERESE. No! I said I wanted *serious* candidates only, and you *promised* you were serious!
(Isaac pulls her close and tries to comfort her.)

ISAAC. Therese, I want to be with you--forever--but I want to be alive for it! We understand each other and that's all we've ever wanted--

THERESE. *(overlapping)* No, no, no, no, no, no…

ISAAC. We can run away and be together--
(She pushes him away and goes over to the kitchen where she takes a knife out and starts carving the roast.)
I mean it! Let's get the hell out of here. We can go anywhere we want.
(Therese puts all her anger into the roast.)

THERESE. Fuck you.

ISAAC. You really need to calm down before someone hears you.

THERESE. I don't give a shit! You said I could trust you!

ISAAC. You can. I do want to give myself to you--just not like *that* anymore. Pack a bag and we'll leave. Tonight.
(Therese waves the hand with the knife in the air, laughing angrily.)

THERESE. Why the hell would I want to start a life with you when I have Toby?

ISAAC. Toby? If you really wanted him you wouldn't have come to me that night! You wouldn't have kissed me--

THERESE. It didn't mean anything! I thought I was doing *you* a favor!

ISAAC. Every time my hand was up your skirt? You thought you were doing *me* the favor?

THERESE. Shut up! Shut up!

(She throws the knife across the room. She then covers her mouth, shocked by her behavior.)

(finding her composure) The only reason I posted that ad… was to live out a fantasy. I never wanted it to be like this. I'm marrying T--

ISAAC. *Oh my God*, if you say that one more time *I'm* going to stab *you*.

(Beat.)

THERESE. So… you really don't want to go through with this?

ISAAC. No… I have you now, and you're worth living for.

(Therese crosses the stage to where the knife landed-- ignoring Isaac's motion to comfort her.)

I'm sorry I couldn't be what you wanted. I've always been told that things are going to get better and I never believed it until I met you. I think I love you, Therese. I'm so sorry.

THERESE. It's fine.

ISAAC. You really do--

(She stabs him. Isaac reels back in pain and confusion. He stumbles and grabs onto the coffee table for support while Therese watches. She stabs him again and again. Isaac falls between the coffee table. Therese watches him as he struggles to hold onto life.)

THERESE. *(comforting)* I know, I promised it wouldn't hurt… but you made promises too, and it's really so much better like this.

(Isaac reaches for Therese, staining her clothes with his

blood before he falls limp.)

You're so beautiful.

(As if in a trance, Therese reaches for her camera on the coffee table and takes a picture of his dead body, and then a selfie. Just for her. So she can remember tonight. She sets the camera down before resting her head on his chest. She's happy. This is love.)

(Beat.)

(Her phone starts ringing. She answers.)

Hi sweetie! How was the flight? Oh well, I'm just glad you guys got there all right… no, nothing much… it's been pretty boring today. Of course you forgot your contact solution… uh-huh… you too. I'll see you on Monday.

(She hangs up and looks around the room and sees the mess she's made.)

Oh shit.

(She walks back over to the body and gasps, covering her mouth. It can't stay there. She crosses to the kitchen to get her a chef's knife. She walks to the body on the floor and debates the best way to take care of it. It doesn't take her long to realize that she can't do it on her own. She pulls out her phone again and, with trembling hands, dials a number.)

(sobbing) Maman? There's been an accident.

Black out.

End of Act I.

ACT II

SCENE 1

Therese is sitting on her couch, an unlit cigarette hangs from her mouth. Her clothing is covered in blood.

His body is still laying on the floor in front of her. There's a knock at the door.

THERESE. *(without looking)* It's open.

(Enter Marie Blanc, Therese's semi-estranged mother. She's dressed as though she just got out of bed.)

MARIE. *(French accent)* What is it? Why did you call me so late?

(She crosses to the front of the couch; she covers her mouth at the sight of her daughter covered in blood and the body on the floor.)

Good God, what did you do?

THERESE. I tried to do it by myself. But, Maman, its eyes are still open? I thought they were supposed to close when you die? Daddy's were closed.

(Marie steps around the body to sit on the couch. She pulls Therese into a hug, an act foreign to both of them.)

MARIE. Shhh, ma poupée, I'm here.

THERESE. I tried to--to take it apart but I couldn't--And then it was staring at me!

MARIE. Now stop that, crying won't clean up this mess you've made.

(Therese pulls away, trying to calm her weeping.)

Let's see a smile.

(Therese forces a smile.)

Good girl.

(Marie stands to assess the situation.)

He's tall isn't he? I don't remember Toby being so tall.

THERESE. It's not Toby, Maman.

MARIE. *(amused)* Not Toby? Oh dear.

THERESE. *(stands)* Don't look at me like that! I met him online and he wanted--

MARIE. Stop! I don't care about that. What are you going to tell the police?

THERESE. There won't be any police.

MARIE. Don't sound so certain.

THERESE. I have everything covered, Mother. No one's going to look for him... he was nobody.

MARIE. Then why call me?

THERESE. Because I don't know what to do when it's *looking* at me! I thought the eyes were supposed to close when you die!

MARIE. The eyelids? Therese, you need to close the eyelids yourself.

THERESE. I can't. It looks sad.

(Marie steps around the body. She kneels down to close the eyes.)

MARIE. Is that better?

THERESE. Help me.

MARIE. With what?

THERESE. I need to get rid of it! It can't still be here when Toby comes home!

MARIE. What were you planning to do with it?

THERESE. We need to cut it up, right? And then I was going to hide him in the woods by the cabin. We were supposed to go to the cabin... before...

MARIE. *(laughs)* No.

THERESE. No?

MARIE. It will attract wild animals, which will lead to someone finding the remains. Honestly, ma poupée you can be so dim.

THERESE. Then what should we do with it?

MARIE. We'll take it to the slaughterhouse tonight. Run it through the grinder.

THERESE. Mother!

MARIE. We won't package it! God. We'll throw it away with the rest of the bad meat.

(Marie picks up the knife on the table and kneels beside the body.)

Between you and I, ma poupée, I would figure out what to say when people come looking for him.

THERESE. No one is going to--

MARIE. Ah-ah-ah, don't take that tone if you want your "maman" to help you. If he came here thinking he'd leave, then someone may end up missing him.

THERESE. He didn't think he would leave. He wanted this.

(Marie glances at the body, raising her eyebrows.)

MARIE. Tomorrow. I want you to go to the police station and tell them you're afraid someone is stalking you.

THERESE. Why?

MARIE. He began stalking you for… whatever reason. So, you wanted a restraining order, but without the evidence, they didn't give you one. If this comes back, you say it was self-defense after the justice system failed you. Get me some garbage bags and something sharp.

(Therese sighs like a petulant teenager and crosses to the kitchen. Marie moves the coffee table out of the way.)

THERESE. I don't want them to know I have any connection to him. *If* someone misses him.

MARIE. You don't have to give a name. Just a man you met online is making you uncomfortable. It's believable.

(Beat.)

So, where *is* Toby?

THERESE. What?

MARIE. Well, he isn't here? So where is he? I'm just trying to make conversation.

THERESE. He's at a conference in Vegas.

MARIE. I see.

(Therese returns to her mother's side with the requested items.)

We should strip... so we don't ruin our clothes...

(She begins removing her clothing. Therese motions to her clothes, already covered in blood.)

We'll have to burn that. Pack a change of clothes before we leave for the slaughterhouse. Lift up the legs. And how is the wedding planning?

(Therese lifts up the body's legs so Marie can slide a garbage bag under them.)

THERESE. I really don't think now is the time to talk about the wedding.

MARIE. Why not? I feel like we haven't spoken in ages. Torso.

THERESE. *(lifting his torso for her mother)* And whose fault is that? You missed our lunch date and dress shopping.

(Marie examines the selection of knives.)

MARIE. What daughter of mine doesn't have a cleaver?

THERESE. We don't do our own butchering.

MARIE. Oh, where did I go wrong? And there's more to a

wedding than lunches and pretty dresses. I always imagined you would have this great, lavish ceremony.

THERESE. We're having a small ceremony at his parent's church.

(Marie is more offended by this than the body on the floor.)

MARIE. Protestant?

THERESE. It's his dream, and we're trying to save money.

MARIE. We *have* money. I'd rather see you married at the courthouse like a common whore.

THERESE. Maman, can we please focus on the task at hand?

MARIE. I am focused. It's wonderful to spend time with my only daughter.

THERESE. Seriously?

MARIE. I am serious. I hate how you've shut me out of your life.

THERESE. I didn't shut you out!

MARIE. Right. Dinner once a month. Phone calls on your time. I want to have a part in your life.

THERESE. You do.

MARIE. An *active* part.

THERESE. Mother.

MARIE. You know, this whole situation is very traumatic. I don't know if I'll be able to keep it to myself. I may need to confide in someone about my daughter…the murderer.

THERESE. Are… are you blackmailing me? That's some real mother of the year behavior.

MARIE. No… I'm asking you to let me be in your life again. A girl needs her mother… for the big moments.

(There's a pause as Therese considers her mother's words. Marie assesses the mess in the living room.)

You're going to need a new rug, we can go shopping tomorrow -- Maybe even get you a new couch to match. Make a girls' day of it.

THERESE. I want to go dress shopping too.

MARIE. Fine, fine. But you better show some gratitude for everything I do for you.

THERESE. Sorry, Maman. I appreciate everything you do for me.

MARIE. Very good, ma poupée. Now let's hurry.

(She takes a knife and hands it to Therese. They kneel by the body.)

No, no cut at the joints -- they're easier to get through than bone.

End of Scene.

SCENE 1b

Enter a hazmat team.
They clean the scene of the crime. Removing the couch and the rug and replacing them with new pieces.
Have fun. This is a dark comedy, after all.
The scene finishes with Marie signing off on a job well done.

SCENE 2

The weekend is over and Marie is true to her word as the apartment is spotless, with a new couch and everything.

Enter toby, home from his Vegas conference. He's taken aback by the new furniture.

TOBY. Therese?

(Therese enters from the bedroom.)

THERESE. You're home!

(She throws her arms around him. She's beaming. Almost like she's a new person.)

TOBY. What happened to the couch?

THERESE. Oh, you'll be so happy to know that Maman and I talked it all out. She's thrilled to help plan the wedding. She was only a little upset about the church situation.

TOBY. Uh-huh… but the couch?

(Marie emerges from the bedroom.)

MARIE. A gift. Therese was bored with the old one.

TOBY. Oh, Marie, hi?

MARIE. I think the sage green would look best on the back wall in the bedroom. It will make the bronze hardware pop.

THERESE. We're changing aesthetics. Everything was so white before, and it's time to bring a little life into this place.

TOBY. You didn't think to call and ask me--

MARIE. *(lighting a cigarette)* Why? It's my apartment.

THERESE. Why don't you take a shower and we'll go out

to dinner? Catch up? Maman wants to throw us an engagement party at the country club.

TOBY. That's nice? Um, we don't smoke in here.

(Marie blows a puff of smoke in his face.)

MARIE. Yes, we're going out to lunch soon with her friend--the short, yappy one--to begin planning.

THERESE. *(leading Toby to the bedroom)* Wren, Maman. Her name is Wren. *(to Toby)* Thank you.

TOBY. For what?

THERESE. Encouraging me to talk to her. A girl really needs her mother for the big moments.

TOBY. So you're saying I was right?

THERESE. Yes, you were right.

(He exits into the bedroom. She lets out a breath.)

MARIE. He's nice, ma poupée. Handsome… trusting.

THERESE. How am I going to do this?

MARIE. Easy, you lie until you start to believe it yourself. Eventually, it'll work itself out.

THERESE. I don't know if I can lie to him.

MARIE. You have to. Do you really think you'd last a day in prison? You're delicate and not very likeable.

THERESE. …I'm likable.

MARIE. Of course. My little ray of sunshine.

(Therese's phone dings.)

THERESE. That's Wren. She's downstairs.

MARIE. Then we should be on our way. This will be fun.

End of Scene.

SCENE 3

Archie is sitting on the couch. He's wearing headphones as he assembles the playlist for the engagement party.

Enter Wren, although she's wearing athletic gear, she's much more put together than the last time she was on stage. However, she's very annoyed as she hauls a giant box with her.

WREN. I *hate* that woman.

ARCHIE. Which one today?

WREN. Both of them. And fuck all if they're actually in the same room.

ARCHIE. All this stress over an engagement party. Can't imagine what the wedding's going to be like.

(She sets the box on the counter and sits next to Archie on the couch.)

WREN. Honestly, Therese is a lot more normal than she should be.

ARCHIE. If you say so.

WREN. Where is she anyway? We were supposed to meet about flowers.

ARCHIE. She's your friend.

(Wren rolls her eyes.)

WREN. She's not as bad as you think she is. She can actually be really fun when you get to know her.

ARCHIE. It's not that she isn't nice, she's just got that creepy rich kid thing about her.

WREN. What does that even mean?

ARCHIE. I don't know. It's like she's already rehearsed

every conversation in her head before it happens. Does something smell like a wet dog?

WREN. Me. It was bath day at the kennel.

ARCHIE. It's good to know they actually bathe you.

WREN. Oh, shut up. From what I hear you're the dog.

ARCHIE. What do you hear?

WREN. Just things.

ARCHIE. So, are there any other members of her family I should know about?

WREN. Most of them are coming in from France and don't speak English, and don't even think of mentioning that new health documentary to her mom.

ARCHIE. Yeah, I already learned that lesson. Where are you staying this weekend?

WREN. Don't worry, I made sure our rooms are on the same floor.

ARCHIE. Excellent.

(He leans over to kiss her as Toby enters the apartment.)

TOBY. Oh come o--Well, this is fine as long as you guys don't break up until after the wedding.

WREN. We're not dating.

ARCHIE. Why ruin a good thing?

TOBY. Hey, as long as you guys keep it quiet, I'm cool with whatever. Is Rese back?

WREN. Nope.

TOBY. *(exiting into the bedroom)* Great. I'm going to take her camera stuff and make a slideshow for the party.

ARCHIE. Have you asked Madame Blanc?

TOBY. *(offstage)* It's my party.

(Enters with the camera.)

I don't need to ask her permission to surprise my bride.

WREN. Vom.

(Therese enters the apartment, on her cell phone. She's dressed in work attire after her office hours at BU. Toby quickly puts the camera back on the counter.)

THERESE. Oui, maman, Wren les a récupérés en chemin..

(She crosses over to the box and opens it. She pulls out a small vase of yellow tea roses.)

Did you change the order? Because I didn't want tea roses. I don't care what you think would look better, it's my party. No, you don't need to come over. Maman? Maman?

(She pulls the phone away from her ear and slams it down on the counter.)

WREN. Is Madame Blanc coming over?

THERESE. Sounds like it.

ARCHIE. Well, I think that sounds like a good reason to head out. Wren, you want to grab some coffee?

WREN. Yeah, I could use a caffeine boost.

TOBY. Guys, wait up!

THERESE. Toby!

TOBY. Sorry, but I was already here for the tablecloth incident. This is one fight I can miss. Love you.

THERESE. You too.

(She waves as they exit. She crosses as though she's about to sit on the couch but stops. She touches it gently then runs a hand over the new rug. She stands, clutching her stomach as though she's about to throw up and crosses to the fridge. She pulls a bottle of wine from the fridge. She grabs a glass and sets both down on the counter. She opens the bottle and gets ready to pour then decides to drink straight from the bottle. There's a knock on the door.)

(too cheerful) Did you forget your keys this time?

(She opens the door to find a man (or woman) standing

at the door. Although he is in his late 40s or early 50s he looks much older.)

DETECTIVE BASS. Therese Blanc?

THERESE. Yes?

(Detective Bass flashes a badge at her.)

DETECTIVE BASS. I'm Detective Daniel Bass. May I come in?

THERESE. Yes, yes, of course!

(Therese instinctively becomes a hostess as she lets Detective Bass enter the apartment. She shuts the door.)

THERESE. Can I get you something to drink? Water? Coke? *(pauses, smirks)* Doughnuts?

(Detective Bass takes a seat on the edge of the couch.)

DETECTIVE BASS. No thank you, I just came to ask you a few questions.

THERESE. About what?

DETECTIVE BASS. You're not in trouble.

(Therese sits in the chair.)

I was brought in to help out with a missing person's case… Isaac Abrams.

THERESE. Oh?

DETECTIVE BASS. I know you tried to file a complaint against someone a few weeks ago?

THERESE. I did, but it didn't go anywhere because I couldn't provide a name.

DETECTIVE BASS. Where did you meet him online?

(Therese straightens her back slightly.)

He had a very interesting Internet history.

THERESE. Well, like every 20-something I'm just obsessed with getting that perfect shot. I'm an amatuer photographer… but my browsing history isn't that interesting. Well, outside of research for my dissertation.

DETECTIVE BASS. Yeah, I try and stay away from all that myself… but the reason I ask is because… well, Mr. Abrams had an account on this… well, I guess the only way to describe it is a fetish website.

THERESE. Oh?

DETECTIVE BASS. And he seemed to have a very close relationship to this one user… Ladyharvester. My colleagues in New York tracked her IP address to this location, and they called me to ask the owner questions.

THERESE. So, you think I'm this user?

DETECTIVE BASS. Well, not at first, but there was also this painting.

(They take out their phone and show Therese.)

And now that I'm sitting here, it does have a striking resemblance.

THERESE. Oh, god. It was worse than I thought. I do have an account on that website. Like I said, I'm writing my dissertation… on consensual murder and connected fetishes, and since you've been on the forum you can understand that it's a cesspool of perfect case studies. And there was one man who responded to my post and we started DMing--direct messaging. It was for research, and I thought he knew that, but he started getting too attached… so attached I just made that report to local authorities about safety concerns… I don't think he knows where I live though.

(There's a moment of silence as he writes it all down.)

DETECTIVE BASS. See, I wanna believe you. You're a pretty girl--The kind every boy imagines taking home to mom. But Ms. Blanc, I read the devouring messages you and Mr. Abrams exchanged, and they don't seem like something a therapist would say to her client. Or "case studies" as you lovingly call them.

(Therese's smile fades.)

THERESE. You read our messages?

DETECTIVE BASS. I did.

THERESE. Those messages were very… personal.

DETECTIVE BASS. Yes, they were. It sounds like there was a lot more to your relationship than just research…

THERESE. I'm engaged. If he were to find out…

(Detective Bass flips a few pages in their notebook.)

DETECTIVE BASS. Then why would you send to Mr. Abrams--

THERESE. Please, I know what the messages said.

(Pause.)

Do I need to get a lawyer?

DETECTIVE BASS. I dunno, Ms. Blanc. Do you think you need one?

THERESE. I feel like you're accusing me of some*thing*. Something I don't appreciate. I'm afraid I'm going to have to ask you to leave. I refuse to answer any more questions without my lawyer present.

DETECTIVE BASS. All right.

(Stands up.)

Thanks for your time, Ms. Blanc. I'll be in touch if I have any other questions.

THERESE. Of course.

(She closes the door behind him and starts biting her thumbnail as she walks over to the counter.)

Fuck!

(She knocks the flowers onto the floor. She kneels down, as if to pick them up but she begins ripping the flowers apart, cursing Isaac as she does. Marie enters, but she doesn't stop her rampage.)

MARIE. You really didn't like the flowers.

(She watches as Therese destroys the flowers.)

THERESE. Everything's wrong. I hate tea roses. I wanted sunflowers.

(She begins sobbing and Marie offers Therese a cigarette.)

THERESE. Not in the apartment, Maman.

MARIE. It's my apartment.

(She hands Therese the lighter after lighting her own cigarette.)

THERESE. *(trying to light the cigarette)* He didn't destroy the painting, Maman. He didn't delete the messages. He never followed the rules. Shit.

(Unable to light the cigarette she throws the lighter on the ground.)

MARIE. Who was that I passed in the hallway?

THERESE. *Detective* Daniel[le] Bass.

MARIE. *Detective*? What did you tell him [her]?

THERESE. I told him what I told you, but he [she] has our messages so he knows it's all bullshit.

MARIE. They don't know that.

THERESE. What am I supposed to say? "Oh, I was just roleplaying to gather intel for my school project?" It sounded so stupid.

MARIE. Maybe. But it's the only true thing you've said about this whole ordeal.

THERESE. Everything is so fucked.

MARIE. Language. Maybe you should have thought about it before you murd--

THERESE. I didn't murder him!

MARIE. Fine, whatever you kids are calling it these days.

THERESE. He wanted it to happen--

MARIE. *(laughing)* Did he?

(Therese doesn't say anything. Marie grabs a box of tissues and drops it to the ground.)

THERESE. He wanted it to happen. I swear, Maman.

MARIE. Clean yourself up.

THERESE. What are you going to do?

(Marie heads toward the exit.)

MARIE. Do what I have always done. Clean up your mess.

THERESE. He didn't mean anything to me, Maman.

MARIE. Apparently, no one does.

End of Scene.

SCENE 4

Later.

Therese is on her hands and knees cleaning the floor around the living area where she had her breakdown. Toby enters the apartment, confused by what he's walked in on.

TOBY. Spill something?

THERESE. Everything's a mess.

TOBY. Looks spotless as always.

THERESE. No, not the apartment. Just. Everything.

TOBY. Cold feet?

THERESE. No… no. I just made a mess with the flowers earlier, and I'm a mess.

TOBY. You're not a mess. You're just stressed.

(He crouches next to her.)

I think I know what this is really about.

THERESE. How could you possibly know?

TOBY. I found them.

THERESE. What?

TOBY. Your cigarettes.

THERESE. My cigarettes?

(She laughs.)

TOBY. I understand you're stressed, but there's better ways to handle it.

THERESE. You're right.

TOBY. You worked so hard to quit.

THERESE. I did.

TOBY. I just don't want to see that all thrown away. Not

when we're so close to the next chapter. I want Marzia and Addison to grow up with a healthy mom.

THERESE. You're right, Toby. You're always right. I'll throw them away before we leave.

TOBY. Good. I'd hate to have to bring one of those cancerous lung posters home.

THERESE. But it would look so wonderful in the bedroom.

TOBY. And if you feel like lighting up again… just remember that this party, this engagement, and this wedding don't matter. All that matters is that we have each other. It's just about you and me.

THERESE. Yeah, just you and me.

TOBY. I hope that makes you feel better.

(Therese turns to him.)

THERESE. I just need to know that you'll want to stay with me. No matter what.

TOBY. Well, that's kinda the point. I don't think I'd still be here if I wasn't planning to stick around.

THERESE. You promise? No matter how bad it gets?

TOBY. I don't see how it could get bad. I put up with all your family drama, and you've been pretty patient about dealing with Mallory. By the way, your mom made her cry yesterday.

THERESE. She makes a lot of people cry.

TOBY. And I'm willing to put up with that because that's what makes a marriage. Whatever happens, we'll work through it. For better or for worse.

THERESE. Maybe we should write our own vows.

TOBY. See, maybe a protestant wedding isn't so bad after all.

THERESE. Yeah, right.

TOBY. I love you.

THERESE. Forever?

TOBY. Of course.

(He stands up and pulls her to her feet.)

Come on, let's go to bed. You'll feel better in the morning.

(Therese heads into the bedroom. Toby quickly grabs the camera off the counter. He looks over his shoulder to make sure Therese hasn't left the bathroom. He starts going through the pictures to make sure it's the right SD card.)

THERESE. *(from the bedroom)* You coming?

TOBY. Yeah, I'm just plugging in my phone.

(Toby's smiling as he looks through the camera. But his expression changes as he gets farther into the photos. At first he's confused, then horrified. He sets the camera down, looking as though he might throw up. He collects himself and slips the camera into his pocket.)

Um, Archie just texted, he left his headphones over here. I'm just going to run them over to him.

THERESE. Oh, okay. I'll see you in a bit then?

TOBY. Yeah, I'll be back soon.

End of Scene.

SCENE 5

It's the night of the engagement party.
Therese is in the kitchen in a white robe, already
in a confrontation with her mother, who's in an
evening gown.

THERESE. Mother, you look fine.

(Marie looks at her reflection in a kitchen appliance.)

MARIE. I think that bimbo went too heavy on the eye shadow.

WREN. *(offstage)* I can hear you!

(Marie crosses the stage and shuts the bedroom door.)

MARIE. I want you to consider coming home. At least for a little while.

THERESE. That was not part of the arrangement.

MARIE. I'm making an amendment. Just until I know I can trust you again.

THERESE. No.

MARIE. Do you know how much convincing and money it took for that detective to drop it? Honestly, drugs would have been a much more affordable cry for attention.

(Enter Archie in a suit.)

ARCHIE. Christ, are you still not ready? Where the hell is Wren?

(Archie exits into the bedroom.)

ARCHIE. The limo's here!

WREN. And I told you I still have rollers in!

THERESE. Toby would never agree to it.

MARIE. You haven't even asked.

(Toby enters.)

TOBY. Marie, the limo's here.

MARIE. So I heard. It'll wait until the bride's ready.

TOBY. Is that what you're wearing?

THERESE. Oh, yes, it's the latest trend in Paris.

(She leans in to kiss him but he turns away.)

I'm waiting for Wren to finish.

TOBY. Yeah. Okay.

(His shortness makes Therese uncomfortable.)

THERESE. It shouldn't take that long to take rollers out. I'm going to go check on them. Can you pack my camera bag?

TOBY. Sure thing.

(Therese exits into the bedroom.)

THERESE. *(offstage)* I just washed those sheets!

(Wren and Archie enter from the bedroom, hair disheveled as Toby packs up the camera bag.)

ARCHIE. We're, um, going to wait in the car.

WREN. Limo.

ARCHIE. Limo.

(They exit into the hallway. Therese closes the bedroom door. Toby sighs and sits on the couch.)

MARIE. You seem… how you say… glum?

TOBY. I just have a lot on my mind.

(Marie sits on the opposite end of the couch and lights a cigarette.)

MARIE. You can tell me. We're almost family.

TOBY. Have you ever found out something you wish you hadn't?

MARIE. Mon chou, I own a slaughterhouse.

TOBY. Right, of course. It's just… I know something that I shouldn't, and I'm not sure what to do.

MARIE. Getting cold feet, hmm?

TOBY. I don't know. I love Therese, I just--

MARIE. You just what?

TOBY. I think marrying her means committing to some other things I don't want to.

MARIE. *(smirks)* Everyone has skeletons in their closet, mon chou.

TOBY. I actually like to keep my closet skeleton free.

MARIE. Did Therese ever tell you about our cat.

TOBY. The one that fell out the window?

MARIE. That's what she says, but… how does a cat open a window? *(sigh)* She's always messy with details.

TOBY. What are you saying?

MARIE. We all have secrets, but that's why we lock them away.

TOBY. I don't think this is something I can just… ignore.

MARIE. It's a difficult world. Are you really going to judge people for what they have to do to survive?

TOBY. Marie--

MARIE. You want a perfect life? A perfect wife? Such luxuries don't come cheap.

TOBY. I don't think--

MARIE. Have you considered what she's willing to give up for your dreams? One must always make a sacrifice to reap the benefits of the American Dream. Tragic but true. Just look at me.

TOBY. Marie--

MARIE. Just something to think about. It would be humiliating if we had to cancel the party because you can't accept the harsher truths.

(Marie puts out her cigarette and rests a hand on Toby's cheek.)

A comfortable life in exchange for a few skeletons

seems fair, no?

(She stands up as Therese re-enters in a white cocktail dress. She does a twirl to show off the dress, then sees the look on Toby's face.)

THERESE. What's wrong? *(to Marie)* What did you say to him?

MARIE. I'll leave you two to talk.

(Marie exits.)

THERESE. What's wrong?

(Toby steps away from her.)

TOBY. Therese, I don't know if I can do this.

THERESE. What are you talking about?

(Toby pulls her camera out of his pocket.)

TOBY. I know.

(He tosses it to her.)

I saw the pictures.

THERESE. You went through my camera?

TOBY. I wanted to make something special for tonight. A slideshow of our "precious memories."

THERESE. Oh God. Toby--

TOBY. Who was he?

THERESE. What--

TOBY. Please don't play dumb, Therese, not now. Who the fuck was he? The guy in the pictures, who was he?

THERESE. It's complicated.

TOBY. Just answer the fucking question, that's all I want.

THERESE. We can talk about this later. We're going to be late--

TOBY. You're worried about the party? Now?

THERESE. *(rambling)* I was researching for my paper, I stumbled across this website where people with weird fetishes can meet and talk. So, I signed up thinking it would be interesting to interview someone like that--well, he just got too attached and when I invited him over for an in-person interview he--he attacked me. It was self-defense, Toby, that's all.

TOBY. Your research?

(Toby pushes over the stack of books that have been living on the counter/table/whatever. Therese has never seen him this angry.)

How the hell do you expect me to believe that *this* is because of some paper.

THERESE. It's not just *some* paper. It's the basis of my career. It's everything I worked for--it's who I am.

TOBY. Who you are? I don't even know who the hell that's supposed to be anymore. A person just doesn't keep a secret this big from their partner. It makes me think there's more--

THERESE. It was too hard--I was embarrassed for being so stupid. I should have known he'd be mentally--

TOBY. I can't listen to this bullshit.

THERESE. What do you want from me?!

TOBY. I don't know. Shit. It's all so fucked up. I want to forget it, but I can't. You took pictures--I can't even wrap my head around that.

THERESE. I wasn't thinking--I was so traumatized I just couldn't think--

TOBY. You looked proud--happy. I don't even know... but I know you weren't traumatized. And I know that I can't do this.

(He heads for the exit.)

I'll tell Arch and Wren to tell everyone the news.

THERESE. You can't.

(She rushes to him and takes his face in her hands.)

Look at me, Toby, look at me. Hey, it's *still* me. Despite

everything I'm still me, and I still want to marry you.

TOBY. Rese--

THERESE. What will you have if you leave me? The apartment is mine. Everything in it. It's all mine.

TOBY. There--

THERESE. Nothing has to change. He meant nothing to me. He was just a research project. Toby, you are my husband. There's *nothing* wrong with *me*--I'm still the girl you borrowed a pencil from--

TOBY. I know it's still you and that scares the shit out of me. I can't marry a fucking serial killer---

THERESE. I'm not a serial killer. One person, Toby. *One.* And it's what he wanted. He came to me. He asked for it. It wasn't murder.

TOBY. Do you hear the words coming out of your mouth right now?

THERESE. I love you.

TOBY. You don't keep secrets like this from someone you love.

THERESE. I fucked up, okay? I was stupid, and I let things get out of hand.

TOBY. Are you sorry?

THERESE. What?

TOBY. You killed someone. I want to know if you feel something.

(There's a pause as Therese shakes her head and slowly crosses over to him.)

THERESE. It's so easy for you to judge me, right? Because you're so goddamn perfect? *(mocking)* "Kissing a smoker is like licking an ashtray, Therese. My mom used to add dill to my eggs, Therese. Running every day is a great way to reduce stress, Therese."

(She laughs.)

You want the truth? Fine. I killed him. I found him online. He wanted to be tortured and killed and I agreed to help him. I stabbed him fifteen times. In this room.

TOBY. I don't understand.

THERESE. Of course you don't. I don't even understand, but I'm trying. I'm trying to connect the dots and figure out why… why there's this itch in my brain.

TOBY. I don't believe this. Do. No. Harm.

THERESE. Do no… how is it doing harm if it's what they want?!

TOBY. Was *that* what he wanted?

THERESE. Ideally… it wouldn't have been as messy. Like I told you, he got aggressive, and I did what I had to. But what does it matter as long as we achieved the desired results.

(Toby crosses to the couch and sits down.)

You're telling me that you've never thought about it? When you see a patient that will have a harder life if you did everything to keep them alive? You never think that maybe… just maybe… the best thing you could do for them is to end it. You have so much power when there's someone under your scalpel. All it takes is one slip.

TOBY. Never.

THERESE. Never?

TOBY. We took an oath to do no harm.

THERESE. Right. I almost forgot how perfect you are. That you would never do anything remotely bad even if it's--

TOBY. Fine. I have thought about it. Terminal patients in the worst pain of their life… Yes, they deserve to end their life on their own terms. And there was this time…

(Beat.)

THERESE. Yes?

(Beat.)

TOBY. Of course there are moments... sometimes I've looked into the faces of patients who are really suffering... the thought crossed my mind. Ending their life would bring them relief--and maybe terminal patients deserve the right to choose what happens to them.

(Therese is excited about the words coming out of his mouth.)

However, at the end of the day, I took and oath. *We* took an oath. To do no harm.

THERESE. But... I didn't do any harm. He was going to kill himself one way or another. It wasn't his first attempt. He just needed someone to help him over the edge. Harm would be forcing him to live a life he no longer wanted. No one chose to be born, so it's only fair that we decide when and how we leave it. You're telling me if a patient was suffering and begged, *begged* for you to end their pain, that you would deny them and let them anguish? He begged me to help him. To *save* him. And I did. Can't you understand?

(Beat.)

(Despite what he saw, she's still the woman he fell in love with. Maybe Marie is right.)

TOBY. *(mumbles)* Just a few skeletons... perfect wife, perfect life.

THERESE. What?

TOBY. I... want to. Because you're you, and I know you, and I love you... and maybe... in some fucked up way... you did just want to help him. But--

THERESE. Let's not think about the "buts" right now. We have our whole lives ahead of us... as long as you stay.

(Beat.)

(Therese's phone dings.)

THERESE. They're waiting. We should go.

TOBY. Was he really the only one?

(Therese sits next to him and rests a hand on his leg.)

THERESE. Of course he was the only one.

TOBY. What did you do with the body?

THERESE. It's better if you don't know. But it's gone. They won't find it.

TOBY. What about his family?

THERESE. He didn't have one.

(Beat.)

TOBY. How can I… can I trust that you won't do that to me.

THERESE. What?

TOBY. If you did it once, what's stopping you from doing it to me?

THERESE. I'm not some psychopath. I don't just sit around all day thinking about killing everyone I meet. It was just one time. One thing I needed to do.

(Beat.)

TOBY. We can't fix this overnight.

THERESE. I know. But I can't do this without you.

TOBY. Do what?

THERESE. Be normal. You're my rock.

TOBY. When my parents said marriage was going to be hard--

THERESE. I love you.

TOBY. *(sighs)* I love you too.

THERESE. Then stay, please. I know things can't stay the same, but we need to try. This was something I had to figure out for myself. I know now you're the only man I want to be with, and the only one who truly understands me. Anyone else would have run the moment they saw those pictures, but you stayed… because I know you *do* understand. Even if you're not ready to admit it.

(Beat.)

TOBY. All right… let's try.

(He offers her a hand and they proceed to the door. She's happy. This is love.)

THERESE. We'll be fine. I promise. Oh! I don't know if I told you, but we changed the fish entrée to pan-seared stone fish with lemon risotto.

TOBY. Oh, I was looking forward to the salmon.

THERESE. And I was looking forward to not getting married in a church and yet…

TOBY. Fine, fine… I'll give the stone fish a try. Marriage is all about compromise, right?

THERESE. That's right. Trust me, it's going to be perfect… not that it has to be.

TOBY. You're right. We're getting married. That's more than enough.

(Toby puts his arm around her shoulders as they exit the apartment.)

Black out.

The End.

NOTES
(Use this space to make notes for your production)

GATHER BY THE GHOST LIGHT is a storytelling podcast in radio theater format. Think of the Ghost Light as your campfire. Gather around and listen to stories from a variety of genres. Playwright Jonathan Cook and Devon McSherry are the hosts of the series and most of the stories you hear were originally written as short stage plays and they now have been adapted to audio plays with professional voice actors and immersive sound effects. The audio plays produced on this podcast give these talented playwrights an even wider audience for their stories. We welcome you to join us in this journey as we extend the voices of emerging playwrights!

Available wherever you get your podcasts!
For more information, please visit:
www.gatherbytheghostlight.com

Gather by the Ghost Light annual anthologies of audio plays produced on the podcast are all available through Ghost Light Publications!

BOBBY IS DEAD

by Marty Matfess

(3M, 2W, Dark Comedy)

Chris has been madly in love with his best friend Annie for years, but she's only been interested in dating everyone else but him. After Annie's recent break up with her boyfriend Bobby, Chris feels this may finally be what he needs to find his way into her heart, but just like that ... she's already moved on to another guy she met at a coffee shop. Being the good friend that he is, Chris has agreed to hang out with the new guy's visiting sister while they go out on a date. Oh, and let's not forget about Bobby. Turns out he's not taking the break up too well and Chris is now caught between an aggressive ex-boyfriend while having to keep new guy's sister company. A play about love, lust, and getting shot in the head.

IN THE SLUSH

by Daniel Prillaman

(2M, 2W, Cosmic Horror)

2023 FINALIST FOR NEW DRAMATISTS' PRINCESS GRACE AWARD

Newlywed Laura Beth Gardner has it all. A loving husband, a baby on the way, and a usually delightful job. But this weekend, tasked with reading through her publishing house's slush pile, she encounters a mysterious manuscript that claims she isn't human. That her husband isn't who he says he is. And that she's a vessel for her unborn child, who is actually the Second Coming of an ancient darkness that will devour the world. It has to be some sort of joke.

…But what if it's not?

A cosmic horror about identity, creation, and the things we'll do to realize our dreams.

Also by GHOST LIGHT PUBLICATIONS

ALL BARK, NO BITE

by Kara Emily Krantz

(2M, 3W, Comedy)

Charlotte and Eugene live a quiet, no-nonsense lifestyle surrounded by sudoku and argyle. Robert and Bella are boisterous and messy and ridiculously in love. Then there's the neighbor, Suzanne, who basically doesn't know what's going on, but definitely has something to say about it. Sure, relationships can be exciting! They can also be confusing, unexpected, and expose us to profound emotional risk. However, relationships are almost always worth exploring, and if we're willing to be vulnerable, can fill up the empty or wounded spaces in our hearts. And if that doesn't work? Well, get a dog.

HUGO SAVES CHRISTMAS…IN MAY!

by Steven Hayet

(1M, 3W, Comedy)

For Maya Kaplan, Christmas is her life… and she hates every minute of it. As acting manager of a year-round Christmas store, Maya is force-fed jolly, subjected to hearing the same holiday songs on loop day after day. Fortunately, Maya's nightmare will be coming to an end in a few months as the store will finally shutter its doors to become a Starbucks. Or will it? Enter Hugo McGee, a longtime customer devastated to learn of the store's closing. Refusing to allow a local intuition to disappear, Hugo makes it his mission to raise the money and keep Yuletide Cheer open, despite Maya's objections.

KINGDUMB

by Jonathan Cook

(10M, 6W, Comedy)

There's a new King in the land that has initiated a mysterious new tax on the citizens. Outraged, the region's finest Clock fixer, aka "Time Repair Specialist", recruits some of the most unlikely rebels to help him develop a plan to overthrow the King. Their plotting takes them on a comedic journey through perilous mountain tops all the way to the palace itself where they confront this vile King face to face. Kingdumb is a medieval fantasy comedy full of absurdist humor and illogical behavior.

THE CHRONICLES OF GREAT BRITAIN'S FIRST EVER VAMPIRE TEDDY BEAR

by Christopher Plumridge

(1M, Comedy, One-Man Show)

This is the story of a Teddy Bear who became a legend! Detailed across ten adventurous monologues, each one more heroic and entertaining than the last. Through his various exploits you will discover how a simple stuffed toy became the legend that is 'Great Britain's First Ever Vampire Teddy Bear'.

VERLASSEN

by Avery Lewis

(2M, 3W, additional ensemble roles, Drama)

A prisoner awaiting his punishment. A pastor seeking vengeance. A survivor searching for peace. All three are looking to one girl, Ida Verlassen, to give them what they're after. As time works against them and revelations are made, Ida must decide who she trusts, and which direction she will choose to go.

BARON OF BROWN STREET

by Eric Mansfield

(9M, 7W (or 4M, 2W with doubling), Drama)

Lenny King, a homeless man living alone in a tent under Akron's Brown Street bridge, becomes an overnight celebrity after a newspaper story details Lenny's kind heart in forgiving three teens who set him on fire and laughed at his pain. Enduring the physical and emotional scars of a man abused by life and his own bad decisions, Lenny must now fend off strangers looking to exploit him for their own publicity and others from his past looking to help him and reconnect. (Inspired by true events.)

THE ROCK AND THE HARD PLACE

by Emily McClain

(4M, 3W, Drama)

Alan Tully was convicted of the murder of Janice Beck in 1996 and has been on death row for 23 years, during which time he has maintained his innocence. His daughter Elsie receives a letter from the man who claims to have committed the crime and she attempts to use the information to exonerate her father. The insurmountable challenges of exonerating a wrongly convicted person drive her to the desperate position of threatening a man she believes could help free her father, with disastrous results.

THE DESTINATION

by Ryan Kaminski

(2M, 3W, Thriller)

In the midst of a blizzard, a group of strangers seek refuge in a secluded motel, unaware that the motel proprietor and a mysterious stranger will make them part of a deadly game. A psychological horror play set during the holiday season.

BETWEEN DOG AND WOLF

by Cris Eli Blak

(2M, 1W, Drama)

2024 WINNER CHARLES M. GETCHELL NEW PLAY AWARD

High school friends Blake, Patrick, and Mara reunite at a hotel the day before their 10-year reunion. Forever traumatized by the school shooting that took place their junior year, the three try and fail to relive painful memories and heal broken friendships.

CRAZY QUILTS

by Karen Fix Curry

(1M, 4W, Dark Comedy)

A young woman goes to interview a quilting group and finds herself being interviewed for inclusion in their exclusive secret club. Things are not always what they seem. Strangers can quickly become family, and at her lowest moment can change her life in unexpected, profound, and sometimes unsettling ways.

www.ghostlightpubs.com